P9-DMR-083

nickelodeon™

Welcome to Alfea

The Junior Novelization

randomhouse.com/kids

ISBN: 978-0-307-97994-0

Printed in the United States of America

10 9 8 7 6 5 4 3 2 1

nickelodeon™

Welcome to Alfea

The Junior Novelization

Adapted by Randi Reisfeld

Random House 🏠 New York

Chapter 1

It was a lovely morning in the city of Gardenia. In a bedroom filled with hand-drawn sketches and colorful clothing, a girl with dark red hair snuggled deeper into the covers. A book with winged creatures on the cover lay half open on the floor next to the bed.

A woman with short brown hair and cheerful brown eyes entered the room. She went to the bed and gently shook the sleeping girl. "Bloom, honey, time to get up."

Through a fog, Bloom heard her mother's voice. Her blue eyes opened.

Bloom's mom, Vanessa, leaned over the bed. "You're going to be late for school, dear."

Bloom glanced at her alarm clock. It was ten o'clock. "Oh, no!" she exclaimed. "Mom, why didn't you wake me earlier? Why didn't the alarm go off?" She bolted out of bed. As her fluffy gray-and-white pet bunny, Kiko, looked on, Bloom washed and dressed in a flash.

It wasn't until she had pulled her blue-and-yellow shirt over her head that she realized something was wrong. Bloom turned and narrowed her eyes at her mom. "Wait a minute—there isn't any school! It's summer vacation!"

Bloom's mom looked amused.

"Not funny," Bloom said, groaning.

"I thought it was funny," Vanessa replied.

"I'm going back to sleep." Bloom jumped grumpily into bed and pulled the covers over her head.

As Bloom shut her eyes, Vanessa asked, "Sweetie, why were you up so late last night?"

"I was reading," Bloom mumbled. Her mom picked up the book next to the bed. She frowned as she read the title.

"Fairies: Myth or Reality?" She looked at her daughter with raised eyebrows. "Pretty silly stuff, Bloom."

"It is not silly!" Bloom protested. Ever since she could remember, Bloom had been interested in fairies. She loved the idea of mythical creatures with magical powers flying around the world doing good. Bloom secretly believed that one day, if she looked hard enough, she would find them.

Bloom's mother headed out the door. "Remember, now that school is over, you can help me in the shop," she called over her shoulder before heading downstairs to cook breakfast.

Bloom winced. Spending long days cooped up in her mom's flower shop was the last thing she wanted to do over summer vacation. With a yawn, she got out of bed and headed to the kitchen with Kiko at her heels. Perhaps she could convince her father to help keep her from being stuck inside the entire day.

"Good morning, sunshine!" Bloom's dad, Mike, lowered his newspaper and smiled up at her.

Bloom crossed her arms. "Dad, I don't want to

spend my summer vacation working in the shop! I wish I could go somewhere fun with my friends."

Her dad said gently, "When you're older, you can go wherever you want, but for now—"

"How old is older?" she asked impatiently. "I'm already sixteen!"

Bloom's dad dodged the question. "Listen, in a few weeks, we will all be going to the beach together, like we do every year."

With a sigh, Bloom tried to explain how she felt. "I don't want to go to the same old beach with you and Mom. I want to do something special."

A mischievous look came into Bloom's dad's eyes. "Well, for that you'll need"—he paused before exclaiming—"wheels!"

Bloom felt her heart race. Could it be? Had her parents really gotten her a car? Holding her breath, Bloom ran through the kitchen, flung open the front door, and dashed outside. There, parked next to the house was a brand-new, shiny red . . .

. . . bicycle.

Bloom's heart sank.

Her parents joined her outside. "Nice, huh?" Her dad beamed. He gestured toward a bright bunch of colorful flowers in the bike's basket.

Bloom swallowed her disappointment. "Uh, well . . . yeah. . . . Thanks!" she said, forcing herself to sound cheerful. She took the bike by the handlebars and steered it down the driveway. Kiko hopped out of the house toward her, and Bloom scooped the bunny into the basket.

As Bloom walked the bike away from her house, she heard her parents talking. "See, she's speechless!" crowed her dad.

"I can see that," her mom agreed. "But I think she was expecting something else."

"A ten-speed?"

"A car, Mike!" Bloom's mom shook her head. "She's sixteen, and she's growing up."

Bloom's dad laughed. "Nonsense. She still dreams about being a fairy."

As Bloom pedaled along the streets of Gardenia,

she thought about what her dad had said. He could be clueless at times, but he was right about her obsession with fairies. Bloom really did wish to become a fairy. It wasn't childish. Fairies were sweet and beautiful, like glittering angels with long hair, fluttering wings, and magical powers. Bloom knew that not everyone believed in fairies. But she did, with all her heart and soul.

Bloom rode her bike to Gardenia Park and stopped at the entrance. Kiko hopped out of the basket and into the grass.

"Okay, Kiko," Bloom called as the bunny bounced toward the woods. "Don't go too far." Leaning the bike against a shady maple, she settled onto the ground. Munching an apple her mother must have packed in the basket, Bloom wondered what it would be like to be a fairy—to have wings and magical powers and save the world from time to time.

Bloom was lost in her daydreams when Kiko hopped out of the woods. His eyes bulged, and his floppy ears stood stick-straight with fear.

"What's the matter, Kiko?" Bloom asked, alarmed.

She had never seen her bunny look so terrified.

Kiko hopped frantically toward her, then pivoted and dashed back into the woods. Bloom got up and followed as Kiko led her deeper and deeper into the trees. The sounds of other people in the park faded away. As Bloom entered a clearing, she got the shock of her life.

CHAPTER 2

In a secluded section of Gardenia Park, a battle was raging. A girl about Bloom's age with long blond hair, dazzling gold bracelets, and wings sprouting from her back wielded a scepter—a tall rod topped by a wheel with spokes. The girl was defending herself against the most bizarre group of creatures Bloom had ever seen.

The biggest was a monstrous mustard-colored ogre, as wide as he was tall, with a big, fat bald head and bushy eyebrows. He was barefoot and dressed only in mud-brown overalls. His hands were clenched into fists, making his intention clear as he advanced on the girl. He wanted to clobber her!

The ogre led a band of bloodred creatures. The

size of giant tortoises, they crawled like crabs, leapt like cats, and struck with knifelike claws. It was their eyes—or, rather, dead white slits where eyes should have been—that gave them away. Ghouls! Bloom shivered.

How could one girl fight them all off?

"Rising Sun!" the winged girl shouted, kicking at the ghouls. One of her sparkling gold bracelets lit up—and shot out a beam of magical energy! Four ghouls disappeared into tiny particles of light. But the giant ogre continued his approach. His huge black eyes burned with hatred.

Bloom gasped, terrified.

The girl fought on bravely, facing the ogre. "I am Stella, Fairy of the Shining Sun! So back off!" she bellowed as a halo of bright light formed around her.

Her words only made the ogre more determined. He charged and crashed into her. Stella was pitched upward. She seemed to hang in midair for a second; then she plummeted to the ground, losing her grip on her scepter.

"I know who you are!" the ogre growled. He called

to his remaining ghouls, "Take her scepter!" One of the ghouls ran to the scepter and snatched it from the ground. The ogre towered over Stella. "Not so sunny now, are you?" He chuckled.

Bloom knew she had to help the girl. As she stepped into the clearing, she felt something strange and powerful come over her. "Let her go!" she shouted.

The ogre turned to Bloom. Rage twisted his face.

Uh-oh. Bloom shuddered. What had she just done?

"Get her!" the ogre roared at his ghouls. The crimson creatures instantly obeyed, heading for Bloom. Her heart racing, blood pounding in her ears, Bloom threw up a hand.

"Get back!" she commanded. A blinding flash of flaming light flew from her fingers and struck the ghouls. They stumbled, then quickly retreated deep into the shadows.

The ogre was astonished . . . and so was Bloom!

"Did I just do that?" she whispered to herself.

In response, an elated Kiko, perched atop a tree

stump, mimed a boxer's stance, punching the air. Kiko was so busy doing his happy victory dance that he didn't notice a ghoul sneaking up behind him! The ghoul reached out with his claws, ready to sink them into the bunny.

"Hands off!" Bloom roared. She grabbed a stick to fend off the ghoul. With a mighty swing, she drove the creature smack into a tree trunk.

Bloom was just about to breathe a sigh of relief when something seized her from behind. The ugly ogre clutched Bloom by her wrists and swung her into the air. "Bad move, little girl," he sneered.

Terrified, Bloom kicked and screamed. She fought off the ogre with a fierce energy she didn't know she had. Suddenly, something inside her broke free, and a tornado-force wind whirled around her. The tornado took the shape of a flaming dragon! The dragon flew upward, then doubled back and opened its mouth. Magical fire shot out of its mouth—directly at the ogre and the ghouls! The ghouls scattered into the woods, and the force of the flame knocked the ogre flat onto his back.

Bloom fell to the ground and watched, astonished, as the dragon flew off into the sky.

Next to her, the strange girl who had called herself Stella sat up. She got to her feet and picked up her scepter, dropped by one of the ghouls. She turned to Bloom. "Wow, you pack quite a punch!"

Exhausted and breathing hard, Bloom had no way to explain what had just happened.

"Hey, thanks," Stella said to Bloom.

"Oh, no problem." Bloom regained her voice just in time to see the ghouls return. They surrounded the ogre and helped him up.

As they all retreated, the ogre growled, "We'll meet again, fairy!" He clapped his hands together and vanished, taking his ghouls with him.

"Wow, that was weird," said Bloom, turning to Stella. She was about to ask Stella about her wings when the fairy collapsed onto the ground. Her wings disappeared. "Oh, no!" Bloom cried. She knelt by the motionless fairy and shook her gently. The girl didn't move.

Bloom didn't want the ogre to return and find the

fairy unconscious, so she made a decision. She quickly ran back to her bike and wheeled it to the clearing. "I have to get you to my house!" she declared, kneeling next to the fallen fairy. Using all her strength, Bloom lifted the fairy onto her bicycle and made her way back home.

While Bloom took Stella safely back to her house, the ogre and his ghouls reappeared in a Magic Dimension. His bosses were not happy. Three pairs of diamond-shaped eyes glistened in the darkness. "Knut, you useless ogre. You have failed," one of the bosses scolded.

"I'm sorry, Your Scarynesses." Knut wrinkled his nose and tried to explain. "It's not my fault. I did everything you asked. I defeated Stella the fairy and got her scepter. But then another fairy showed up. She was super-powerful and fought with flames that turned into a dragon. I had to leave the scepter behind, or she would have destroyed me!"

"A super-powerful fairy with the power of the

Dragon Flame?" mused another of the trio. "How interesting."

"We must find out more about this mysterious fairy who can command the Dragon Flame," said a third voice. "Knut! This time we're sending you back with some help. Girls, shall we summon a troll?"

"Yes, let's do it!" laughed the first voice. "Knut and a troll should be able to bring that fairy to us. Let us begin the summoning spell!"

Voices muttered and cackled, and Knut's eyes grew wide as he watched a giant blue figure appear from a cloud of smoke.

Chapter 3

"I don't get it," said Bloom's father, scratching his head. "Tell me one more time."

It was evening, and Bloom stood in front of her mom in dad in their living room. Stella was asleep on the sofa next to Kiko.

Bloom again tried to explain what had happened, even though she knew how crazy it sounded. Bloom pointed at Stella, who was beginning to awaken. "Monsters attacked her in the park. And she fought them with some kind of magic! And so did I!" Reliving the battle, Bloom flushed with excitement, only to be brought back down to earth by a scowl from her disbelieving dad.

"Bloom, this is nuts!" he declared. "I think we

should call the police and take this girl to the hospital!"

A voice piped up from the sofa, weak but determined. "Please, don't tell anyone."

Bloom's mom bent to check on the girl. "She's coming to. How do you feel, dear?"

Carefully, the girl lifted herself up. Her eyes brightened a bit. "I'm all right. Thanks for helping me," she said to Bloom. She looked around the room at the three people peering curiously at her. "My name is Stella."

"Hi, Stella!" Bloom chirped. "My name is Bloom."

"Should we call your parents, Stella?" asked Bloom's mom.

Stella smiled. "I don't think you can. I'm not from around here." She paused. "Have you ever heard of Solaria? It's a kingdom far, far away. In the Magic Dimension. I'm a fairy, you know."

Bloom's dad looked at her and her mother and circled his finger next to his ear. His meaning was clear: something was very wrong with this stranger.

Stella ignored Mike's look of disbelief and continued. "So, I was forced down here when this ogre and these ghouls attacked me—"

"Oh, for goodness' sake!" Bloom's dad cut her off. He marched over to an old-fashioned phone and picked it up. "She's delirious. I'm calling the police."

Stella sighed and pointed a finger at the phone. The base of the phone swiftly turned into a cabbage, and the receiver into a carrot.

Bloom's dad jumped.

"Believe me now?" Stella asked.

Bloom smiled. "I believe you, Stella."

Stella's eyes darted from Bloom to Bloom's mom, and then to her dad. "As I was saying, I was being attacked by these monsters—and your daughter showed up and saved me!"

Bloom's parents looked bewildered.

"Actually, I don't know what I did," Bloom confessed.

"A fairy doesn't need to know," Stella said. "She just does it, that's all!"

"Me? A fairy?" Bloom felt as if the room were spinning.

Stella nodded. "I'd say so. I mean, if you throw up energy shields like a fairy and beat down monsters like a fairy, you must be a fairy!"

Bloom's dad stared at the cabbage and the carrot in his hands. He shook his head. "This is just nuts!" he declared. "Totally nuts!"

After dinner, Bloom took Stella on a tour of the house. As they entered Bloom's bedroom, Stella exclaimed, "Oh, I love your room!"

Bloom beamed at the compliment. She took special pride in her room, especially the walls, which were covered with her original drawings. Some depicted her hometown of Gardenia—its skyline, wide streets, and old-fashioned homes. Others were colorful pictures of fairies.

"Wow! Did you draw all these?" Stella asked, examining each one up close.

Perched on the edge of her bed, Bloom nodded shyly.

"I'm being kind of nosy, aren't I?" Stella said, a little embarrassed.

"No, it's okay, Stella." Bloom was flattered. As she gazed at her new fairy friend, it hit Bloom that Stella looked different from before. For a moment, she couldn't figure out why. Then she saw it. In battle, Stella's bright orange outfit had sparkled and she'd had wings. Here in Bloom's room, the wings were gone. Stella's clothes were still cool, but they didn't twinkle.

Bloom recalled what had happened in the park and stared at her hands. Her brow furrowed. "I still can't believe what's happening to me," she said. For as long as she could remember, all she'd ever wanted to be was a fairy. And now a real one, Stella, was in her bedroom, telling her that was exactly what she was. "I wish I could believe that I'm a fairy."

"You are!" Stella was positive. "You can call up your powers when you need them."

Bloom looked doubtful.

"You've always had them," Stella assured her. "You just didn't know it!"

As if to prove it, Stella went to Bloom's desk and waved her hands over a jar of colored pencils. One by one, the pencils slowly rose to hang in midair.

"All you have to do is concentrate," Stella said matter-of-factly.

Bloom watched, transfixed, as the colored pencils

came together and twisted into one supersized pencil with pink spirals and a rainbow tip. It hovered over the desk, looking like an enormous candy stick.

"Okay, Bloom! You try it. Bring them back to their original shapes," Stella said.

Bloom stretched her arms forward and then pointed at the chunky candy-cane-striped pencil Stella had created. If Bloom really was a fairy, she reasoned, breaking it apart into a dozen individual colored pencils should be easy.

It wasn't.

The supersized pencil plopped onto the floor.

Bloom frowned. What had she done wrong? Determined to try again, she pointed at it and silently commanded, *Come on, get up, untangle!*

Still nothing. Bloom kept at it, but the stubborn thick pencil stayed put. Deflated, Bloom groaned. "Oh, man!"

"You just need training," Stella told Bloom confidently as she waved her hand and magically turned the giant pencil into a bunch of individual pencils. With another swipe of her hand, she sent them back into the jar. "And the best place to get it is at the Alfea College for Fairies. That's where I'm going this year." Stella tapped her finger thoughtfully against her lips. "You should go there, too!"

Bloom couldn't believe her ears. None of her books about fairies had mentioned a school specifically for training fairies. "Where is Alfea?" she asked.

"It's on Magix," Stella explained. "That's a planet in the Magic Dimension, home to all the magical creatures in this universe."

Chapter 4

Unbeknownst to Bloom and her fairy friend, trouble was brewing nearby. As night came to Gardenia, a gust of wind swirled the crackling leaves of an old oak a few streets down from Bloom's house. When the wind died down, lightning split the charcoal sky, illuminating a creepy gang of creatures that had appeared out of nowhere.

"Ah, here we are!" Knut the ogre announced. Four fighting ghouls and another monster, a troll, surrounded him. The troll was twice the size of Knut. It was horrible to behold—blue-hued, black-haired, and blubbery. Two pointy fangs protruded from his bottom lip. "Troll! Find that girl!" Knut shouted.

The monster gave a howl. He lifted his head and

sniffed the air, hunting for Bloom. "I smell them. . . . Two fairies!" he grunted, lumbering down the street.

Knut grinned. "We'll take care of both of them!" he crowed. He gathered the ghouls and crept steadily toward Bloom's house, following the massive troll.

No one in Bloom's house had any idea what was about to happen to them.

Bloom's parents were in the living room, trying to make sense of Stella. Bloom's mom was more open to the possibilities than her dad.

"It isn't ridiculous, Mike; it's true!" Vanessa said. "That Stella is not just a normal kid!"

Mike had no comeback. He didn't believe in magical beings, but he had no idea how to explain Stella, who had turned the phone into a vegetable sculpture right before his eyes.

"Stella's magical," Vanessa declared, "and maybe Bloom is, too."

As Vanessa and Mike discussed Bloom, Kiko hopped past them and into the kitchen, hoping to see some dinner crumbs on the floor. Finding nothing, he leapt up onto the kitchen table and was sniffing around when he glanced at the window. He gave a frightened squeal and hurtled off the table and into the living room. He hopped up to Vanessa and Mike and started dancing in panic. "Not now, Kiko—we're really busy," Mike said, shooing Kiko away.

Kiko was not giving up. He grabbed Mike's trouser leg between his teeth and tried to pull him to the kitchen window. When that didn't work, the resourceful rabbit sank his teeth into Vanessa's pants. But it wasn't Kiko's frantic warnings that got Bloom's parents to pay attention.

It was the noise. Deep rumbling, growling sounds came from the kitchen. Irritated, Mike jumped to his feet. "Hey, what's going on back there?" he demanded.

An enormous blue troll with black hair appeared in front of him. *"Rrrrrahhgh!"* he roared.

"Uh-oh" was all Mike could manage. He and Vanessa backed up.

The troll pitched himself forward. He was too big to fit through the archway between the kitchen and the living room. With a mighty shove, he burst through the wall, making a troll-shaped hole. Mike and Vanessa fled up the stairs. The troll flung himself at the sofa where Stella had been sleeping only an hour before and punched the cushions. The cushions burst open and springs went flying. A cloud of dust filled the room as Knut and his four bloodred ghouls entered from the kitchen.

"Where are those little fairies?" Knut thundered.

"Looking for *moi*?"

The evil creatures turned toward the voice. Stella stood poised and confident at the top of the stairs.

"Whaaat?" Knut said.

"I'm right here, you blimp!" Stella taunted. She jumped down the stairs.

Knut, though not the brightest ogre, realized he had been insulted. "Hey, did you call me a blimp?"

"Well, if the shoe fits . . ." Stella shrugged. Then she got down to business. As the troll advanced, she transformed into a fairy, sprouting wings and sparkles. Aiming her first bolt of lightning straight at the troll's midsection, she cried, "Burning Sun!" Her magic was powerful, but it wasn't enough to defeat the troll. With an *"Oof!"* and an *"Aargh!"* he simply staggered backward.

"Don't just stand there!" Knut yelled at the troll. "Get them!"

A pair of ghouls planted themselves on the troll's wide shoulders. Bloom raced to Stella's side. There was no time to lose—she had to help Stella defeat these magical bullies!

"Bloom, we're outnumbered," Stella said. "We're going to have to split them up."

"Ghouls!" Bloom summoned the bloodred, crablike creatures. "Let's take this outside!" She turned on her heel, and the ghastly gang followed. Bloom wasn't scared. But she was nervous. She'd created a diversion by leading the crab crew outside but hadn't planned what to do afterward.

The ghouls seemed to know.

They lined up—one, two, three, four, ready to attack.

Now Bloom was scared.

Just then, a large cooking pot came out of nowhere.

It bounced between Bloom and the lineup of ghouls, forcing the fearsome foursome to stop in their tracks.

Startled, Bloom bent and peeked inside the pot. There was Kiko, his eyes bulging! The rabbit had tried to help by getting between Bloom and the ghouls, but he looked more petrified than Bloom felt!

The ghouls got ready to attack again. Suddenly, something humongous splattered right on top of them. Knut the ogre had been sent flying, courtesy of Stella's fairy power.

Unfortunately, Stella herself followed Knut outside, tumbling through the window. The troll had thrown her out the window!

"Yikes!" gasped Bloom as she watched her friend hit the ground. She rushed to Stella's side, but the golden-haired fairy was far from finished.

"Don't worry," Stella told Bloom. "I've got everything under control. You'll see."

Just then, a shadow covered Stella and Bloom. The troll had bashed his way through the back door and was advancing toward the girls.

Bloom's heart thudded. They were surrounded by

the ghouls, which were slowly closing in on them. Knut had been knocked out, but it was only a matter of seconds before he would regain consciousness. And now there was a huge troll coming for them! In a minute, he'd be upon them. There was nowhere to go. Stella and Bloom were done for!

Chapter 5

Just as the troll was about to strike, a gate appeared out of thin air. It swung open to let four teenage boys through. All wore blue-and-white uniforms with capes and boots.

A rope lasso flew at the troll and wrapped itself around his giant neck like a noose. The troll was trapped!

A redheaded boy wearing glasses and carrying a ray gun called out, "Guys, I'm ready!"

"Okay! Now let's take him to jail, where he belongs!" shouted a boy with shoulder-length blond hair. He held a kite-shaped shield in front of him.

A boy with maroon-colored hair held on to the

rope lasso that had trapped the troll. The troll was tugging hard at it, trying to escape.

"Relax," the boy told his friends, "I've got him completely secured."

"Oh, I'm totally relaxed," said the fourth one, who had light brown hair and was wielding a long sword. "It's you I'm worried about!"

He had reason to be. The tug-of-war between the troll and the teenage boy had just shifted in the wrong direction. The monster yanked the boy right off his feet and shook free of the lasso. With a scream of fury, it descended upon all four boys.

"Stay behind me!" the boy with the shield shouted to his friends. He held it up to the troll, who took a giant swipe at it. The shield shone with power as the troll battered away at it furiously.

Bloom worried that the shield wasn't big or strong enough to stave off the troll.

But the shield held, and the harder the troll went at it, the more brightly it shone. It weakened the monster just enough for the boys to team up. Using their combined magic, they created a crater-sized hole in the ground that swallowed the troll.

The troll was defeated, but there were still four ghouls and one ornery ogre left. Knut had regained consciousness and came roaring toward Bloom and Stella.

Stella and Bloom had had enough. They aimed a double-dose bolt of fairy magic at the ogre's back. It sent him sprawling.

"And that's how you get rid of an ogre!" Stella declared.

Bloom could hardly believe she'd helped. "Wow, I really can do that," she said with awe.

"Totally. I told you!" said Stella.

The stubborn ogre tried one more time to get up, only to be quickly knocked back to the ground by the four mysterious boys. With a groan, he disappeared in a whirl of light, along with the crablike ghouls.

"Bloom," Stella said as she marched up to the guys, "let me introduce you to the Specialists!" She pointed to the maroon-haired lasso expert. "This is

Riven." The boy seemed a little embarrassed by his loss in the tug-of-war with the troll. He ducked his head and mumbled a greeting.

Stella turned to the redhead with the ray gun. "This is Timmy." Timmy smiled shyly.

"Hello!" said the blond with the glow-in-the-dark shield. "I'm Prince Sky." He gave Bloom a big grin.

Bloom's heart fluttered. She found herself grinning back at him.

"And this is Brandon." Stella's voice softened as she indicated the light brown–haired boy who carried the sword.

"Hey," said Brandon to Bloom—but his eyes were on Stella.

While the introductions were being made, the troll reappeared. Somehow he'd climbed out of his underground prison, and Timmy was the first to notice. He shouted, "Hey, you—where do you think you're going?"

The Specialists created rings of energy that coiled around the beast and sent him flying helplessly through the sky. With their mission accomplished, the boys got ready to leave. "See you girls later!" they said in a chorus.

Bloom beamed with excitement. She'd just met four of the most amazing guys on . . . er, not exactly earth, that was for sure!

CHAPTER
6

Back inside the house, Bloom's father was sweeping up the mess left by the troll. As Bloom and her mom went upstairs to discuss fairy school, Stella remained downstairs, inspecting the damage to the house. It was extensive. There were cracks in the walls and a huge hole in the floor. Furniture and pillows were scattered across the living room. Chairs were overturned, and the sofa was completely destroyed.

"Let me help you," Stella said to Bloom's father. "I can fix everything with a little magic."

"Thanks, Stella," Mike said with a sigh, "but I think I'll do it the traditional way." He could no longer deny that something extraordinary had happened. But he still wasn't ready to fully accept it, or Stella's offer of magical housekeeping.

Upstairs in her room, Vanessa had decided that the best thing for her daughter would be to learn magic at Alfea College. After she talked things over with Bloom, the two of them got to packing. A little while later, they went downstairs. Bloom carried a pink suitcase.

"So you're sure about this, sweetie?" her father asked.

"Yes, Dad." Bloom's heart filled with love for her parents. She was going to miss them terribly. "I've got to learn how to use my powers—to be a fairy."

"I know," Mike agreed, trying to sound lighthearted. "But we don't know anything about Alfea College. So"—he paused, seeming to make up his mind—"we're coming with you!"

"Really?" Bloom was thrilled. She wasn't quite ready to leave them, either. "Well, okay!"

"You're not going to a 'Magical Dimension' until we check it out," Mike said as he grabbed his jacket.

"Can we all go, Stella?" Bloom asked, picking up Kiko and holding the bunny close.

At first Stella looked doubtful. Then she said, "Of course. I can bring everybody." Bloom, her parents, and Kiko breathed a sigh of relief.

Stella removed a gold ring from her finger and tossed it high in the air. When it came back down, the ring had been transformed into a scepter. "Ready?" Stella asked.

"Ready!" Mike answered.

"Then let's go!" Stella exclaimed, leading the way outside. Using her scepter, Stella drew a circle in the ground. As everyone stood inside it, the circle glowed brightly with magical energy.

Suddenly, they were all floating through the air! Bloom felt weightless, like an astronaut in outer space. She wasn't scared at all. It was the most amazing feeling. She had no sense of time or direction. After a while, below them, she noticed rolling hills, green valleys, tall evergreen trees, placid ponds, and sparkling lakes. The scene resembled a postcard—or something she herself might have drawn.

Before long, they landed.

Bloom was awestruck. "So this is a real Magic

Dimension!" she whispered. Nothing she'd read about it could compare with the real thing. Far ahead of them, she could just about make out a horseshoe-shaped, pastel-hued complex with arched doorways and tall, high windows. A towering castle in the middle of the complex soared over all the other buildings. Students were already streaming in through a gate at the entrance.

"That's Alfea College," said Stella, pointing toward the cluster of buildings.

"Wow, I've never seen anything like it!" Bloom's father shook his head in disbelief and started off toward the school.

He didn't get far.

Mike stopped dead in his tracks and bounced backward, as if an invisible wall had stopped him. Puzzled, he got up and marched forward again, with the same result. "I can't get through!" he cried, frustrated and confused.

Bloom caught up with her dad but passed through the invisible barrier. Kiko hopped alongside her. "It's not stopping Kiko," Bloom pointed out. She was several feet ahead of her parents, who were both stuck. Bloom turned to Stella.

"Stella, why can't my parents get through?"

Stella shook her head. "I completely forgot! There's a protective barrier that keeps nonmagical creatures out of Alfea." She pointed to the spot where Mike and Vanessa had been stopped. Magical sparks flew from her fingertips. The sparks illuminated a transparent wall blocking Vanessa and Mike.

"I'm sorry," Stella said gently, "but you can't go any farther."

Bloom bolted back to her parents. Her big blue eyes filled with tears. "Mom . . . Dad" was all she could choke out.

"I guess it's time to say goodbye, Bloom." Vanessa's voice caught in her throat.

Impulsively, Bloom ran back and threw her arms around her mom.

"Our sweet girl," Vanessa murmured, wiping a tear away with the back of her hand.

Bloom's dad pulled himself together. "Do your

best, Bloom . . . and remember, whatever happens, you can always come home!" He turned to Kiko. "Kiko! Keep an eye on her!" The rabbit seemed to understand. He sat up on his hind legs, and with his right front paw, saluted Mike.

Stella, moved by the display of family love, gently reassured them. "Don't worry, she's in good hands!"

In the distance, a bell sounded. Then another one rang, followed by a series of bells ringing.

"Come on, we have to go," Stella whispered urgently.

"I'll be home for a visit as soon as I can," Bloom promised her parents.

Stella turned to them. "Okay, you guys, ready? Don't move." She took off her ring and tossed it into the air. "Ring of Solaria!" she cried. The ring reappeared in the shape of a scepter. Stella used her magic this time to create a doorway. "Have a nice trip!"

Bloom watched her parents disappear through the doorway. Part of her wanted to call, "Wait! I'll go with you." But she knew they were going to arrive safely at home. They would miss her and she would miss them, but deep in her heart, she knew she had made the right decision.

Chapter 7

"Here we are: Alfea College," Stella announced proudly.

"This place is incredible!" Bloom marveled at the dozens of teenage girls streaming into the giant front hall. All the girls were decked out in cute, colorful clothes. Bloom wondered if there was a dress code for fairies-in-training. She held Kiko tightly in her arms, still not believing she was going to fairy school!

Stella suddenly leaned in and whispered, "Uh-oh. Trouble! It's Griselda."

A severe-looking middle-aged woman with chin-length dark hair marched up to them. She eyed Bloom suspiciously. "Who are you and where do you think you're going, young lady?"

Bloom tensed. Before she could answer, another woman stepped up to Griselda. She wore big hoop earrings and half-moon glasses low on her nose. Her hair was white and fluffy, as if a gentle cloud had settled on her head. The woman said pleasantly, "Griselda! I see you have found our newest student, Bloom. She'll be part of our new freshman class."

Griselda frowned. "But she's not on the list, Headmistress Faragonda."

The headmistress smiled warmly. "Every fairy is on my list, Griselda. So . . . welcome, Bloom, and"— she raised her voice a touch—"welcome, all . . . to Alfea!"

At the sound of her voice, dozens of student fairies gathered round. The headmistress addressed them. "Let's begin our orientation session, by the end of which we should all know each other better. Becoming a fairy is hard work. But I know that everyone here can do it! Keep in mind that the teachers and I are always here to help you."

Students chatted excitedly to one another as the headmistress's voice changed from formal to friendly.

"Okay! Enough with the boring stuff. Feel free to explore your surroundings, but be very careful. There are dangers lurking about."

Stella leaned over to Bloom. "Headmistress Faragonda always says the same thing to new students." She pitched her voice in a perfect imitation of the headmistress's voice. "'Stay away from the witches of Cloudtower!'"

"Stay away from the witches of Cloudtower!" the headmistress said.

Bloom started to giggle, but a snappy hand clap from Griselda stopped her. "So, girls . . . you are free until tomorrow morning," the dour-faced assistant headmistress said. "You can go to your rooms."

"Good luck, everybody," Headmistress Faragonda said. "I'll see you all tomorrow. Oh! Classes start at eight o'clock sharp. Do be punctual."

"Faragonda is the best," said Stella as she strode confidently along the corridor. Wheeling her suitcase with Kiko hopping in front of her, Bloom kept up as best she could. "But Griselda, ugh."

Bloom had something else on her mind besides

the headmistress and her stern assistant. "Hey," she said to Stella's back, "what's Cloudtower?"

"Magix has three schools," Stella explained, stopping to look at Bloom. "Alfea, our college, is one of them. Redfountain is the college for Specialists. Remember those boys who helped us with the troll and the ogre? They were from Redfountain."

How could I forget? thought Bloom. The Specialists—Riven, Timmy, Brandon, and that friendly Prince Sky—had been amazing!

"Redfountain's headmaster is Saladin," Stella continued. Her voice dipped low. "And the third school is Cloudtower. It's for witches. Scary old Miss Griffin runs it. And some of those witches are really mean."

"How mean?" asked Bloom.

"You don't want to find out." Stella stopped in front of a set of double doors. She pointed at a sign that listed the names of the girls who would be living there. "Hey, look!" Stella exclaimed. "We're in the same apartment! Cool!"

Without hesitation, Stella swung open the doors and walked inside. Bloom followed with her luggage and found herself in a suite of three bedrooms that shared a small sitting area.

"I think that's mine," said Stella, pointing to one of the rooms. She went inside.

"You've got your own room?" Bloom asked, surprised. She'd thought students at boarding schools and colleges had to share bedrooms.

Bloom wandered into the room next to Stella's, wondering whether it might be hers. A huge climbing ivy sat in the middle of the floor. She walked toward it and instantly thought she'd tripped an alarm, because a piercing "Yeeeek!" made her clap her hands over her ears. She looked around frantically, trying to find a switch to turn off the sound.

"Ow, ow, ow!" Bloom heard someone say.

Bloom looked down. She had accidentally stepped on a long, thick vine that stretched across the floor. The vine was attached to the climbing plant. The flower at the top of the plant had opened and was screaming! Feeling terrible, Bloom instantly lifted her foot. The potted plant inched over toward the squished vine and blew softly on it.

"Sorry!" Bloom blurted—to the plant.

She turned at the sound of footsteps. A lovely girl with cascading layers of light brown hair approached and extended her hand. "No, excuse me! I should have warned you that my plant is very sensitive. I'm Flora. I think we're roommates." She bent over the plant and tickled it. "And this is my talking plant! It's a magical creature."

The plant giggled.

Bloom took a deep breath. This whole magic thing was going to take some getting used to. "Well, okay," she said, "I'll just let you and your magical plant get settled." She backed out of the room cautiously. As she did, she ran right into another student.

The girl had cropped magenta hair cut in jagged layers. Luckily, Bloom had not hurt her.

In a clipped voice the girl announced, "Walking backward is irrational. I'm Tecna."

Just then, Stella came over. "Hi, Tecna! I'm Stella."

"And I'm Flora," said the owner of the magical plant.

"I think I have a roommate. Is it one of you?" Tecna looked from one to the other.

At that moment, someone across the room coughed. Bloom, Stella, Tecna, and Flora turned to see who was there. A cute pigtailed girl stood in the doorway, her hand on a suitcase. Earbuds dangled around her neck. She smiled. "I'm Musa," she said in a sweet, musical voice.

Bloom calculated: five roommates living together in one amazing suite. In spite of stepping on Flora's magical plant and bumping into Tecna, she was excited. These girls weren't just any roommates. They were fairies! She tried to push away the tiny doubt that bothered her: Do I really fit in?

CHAPTER 8

After the introductions had been made and each girl had settled in, Stella asked, "Hey, anybody hungry? We could go to Magix City for lunch."

"Cool. We can get to know each other." Flora was all for it.

So was Bloom. "Anyone for pizza?" she suggested.

The four roommates gave her a curious look.

"Pizza?" Musa asked.

"What's pizza?" Flora wanted to know.

Were they kidding? Bloom formed a triangle with her fingers. "You know, pizza?"

Nothing. No sign of recognition.

Okaaay. Pizza it was not going to be.

A short while later, Bloom found herself gazing

out a window of the bus at Magix City in the distance. Everything was so pretty! Bloom had never seen such brilliant colors. She felt like she was in a dream.

When they reached Magix City, Bloom gasped in amazement. It was like a normal city, with buildings and streets and pedestrians, only everything seemed brighter and more colorful. The girls got off the bus at the town square, which had a bubbling fountain right in the middle of it.

It was a beautiful sight, but Bloom suddenly felt a stab of homesickness. She was in a strange world bathed in colors she had never seen before, where no one knew about pizza. "Would it be okay if I called my parents before we ate? I don't want them to worry about me," Bloom said to her new roommates.

"Of course!" Stella replied cheerfully. "We'll wait right here until you return."

Bloom found a telephone booth around the corner and dialed home. Her mom was relieved to hear from her. After reassuring her mom that she was fine, Bloom told her that friends were waiting and she had to go. "Classes start tomorrow morning," Bloom said, "but don't worry, I'll keep you posted."

Bloom's mom held her on the phone a moment longer. She reminded Bloom that she could always come home if she wasn't happy, that she should work hard in school and do her best—the usual stuff. Bloom listened, but her eyes wandered. Suddenly, so did her thoughts.

The movements of a shadow sneaking around the corner caught her attention. There was something very familiar about its hulking size, shape, and lurching movements. Bloom's danger radar went off. It's that ogre that attacked us in Gardenia! she thought.

Bloom rushed to get off the phone. "Um, Mom, I've got to go now, my friends are calling me, so give a big hug and kiss to Daddy for me, please. Bye!"

Keeping the ogre's shadow in sight, she hung up before her mom could protest. The ogre was now pressed against the side of a building, peering around the corner. Bloom's friends were at the fountain just on the other side—exactly where the ogre was facing. He glanced around as if to make sure that no one saw him.

The ogre was spying on Bloom's friends! She had to get back to the fountain and warn them. Bloom crept toward the ogre, ducking behind trees and bushes so he wouldn't see her. She was making good progress when a sudden noise forced her to take cover. She waited until the noise quieted, then peeked out from her hiding place.

"Huh?" she said aloud. The ogre was nowhere to be found! Bloom, out in the open now, looked up and down the street and around the corner. Her friends were still at the fountain, chatting away. Bloom frowned. "Where did that ogre go?" she whispered. "I've got to find him!" She raced down the street, looking left and right. Suddenly, she gasped and stopped. The ogre was in an alley, talking to someone Bloom couldn't see.

"Knut! Did you find her?" a fearsome voice demanded.

"Uh, no, Your Nastyness, but I saw that other fairy—"

Bloom ducked behind a row of trash cans just as Knut moved aside, and she spotted three figures next to him.

Witches!

Bloom had only gotten a glimpse, but she knew she was right. She tried to get a better look, but the alley was narrow and Knut was not. Her view was blocked by Knut's enormous girth.

Bloom's hearing was just fine, however.

A new voice rang out with a warning. "Sisters! We are being watched!"

"May I take care of it?" Someone else spoke up, sounding decidedly devious. A chill ran down Bloom's spine. Frustrated, she whispered, "Move, you big oaf! I can't see a thing!"

Chapter
9

As Bloom craned her neck, trying to get a better look past Knut, something—or someone—came upon her from behind. Before she could turn around, a bright light stunned her, and a powerful jolt lifted her in the air and sent her flying. She landed hard on the ground.

Bloom raised her head, her heart pounding. She was trapped in a dark alley with three menacing witches who were about her age. One was in front of her and another was behind her. An angry ogre loomed above.

"Surprise!" snarled a witch with silver hair and gobs of indigo eye makeup.

Bloom shook.

"So, did you like our little joke?" asked a second witch. This one had greenish hair and catlike eyes.

Joke? If this sort of thing was considered a joke in Magix City, Bloom was ready to head back to Gardenia.

"Look behind you," ordered a third witch. This one had bushy purple hair and wore stiletto-heeled boots.

Bloom obeyed.

"Hey there! Hee, hee, hee!"

It was the same green-eyed witch—she had a double? It took a minute, but eventually Bloom figured it out. There were only three of them. Somehow one had conjured a double of herself. It was the double who had sneaked up on Bloom.

Now a trio again, the witches glared down on Bloom maliciously. How was she going to get out of this mess? Then she heard Stella's voice in her head. *You can do anything! You're a fairy!*

With all the courage she could muster, Bloom summoned her own magic to cast a fairy spell on the witches. "I'm a fairy! Get back!"

Except for a drizzle of sparks from her fingertips, nothing happened.

The witches laughed.

"You call that magic?" hooted the silver-haired witch. In a flash, she raised her arms and unleashed freezing-cold ice crystals in the alley. "Icy says *this*"— a cascade of icicles formed around Bloom—"is magic!"

Icy may have been mean, but she wasn't wrong. Bloom was trapped inside a block of ice!

"Darcy says *this* is magic!" cried the greenish witch who'd clobbered Bloom from behind. She cast her own spell. It was strong enough to break the ice and catapult Bloom to the other end of the alley, where she landed on the ground again.

"Oh, no," she groaned, knowing the third witch, with the purple hair, had yet to strike.

"And Stormy says *this* is magic!" Out of nowhere, a cyclone whirled across the alley—straight toward Bloom. She couldn't escape it. The cyclone lifted her fifty feet into the air, twirling her around next to a high-rise building. Somehow, Bloom managed to grab onto a windowsill and free herself from the raging wind.

She looked down; the three witches and Knut stared up at her. That was when Bloom realized she had a bigger problem than the cyclone. She was twelve stories high, hanging from a building by her fingers! Below, her enemies were mocking her. Where were her friends? Surely they must be missing her by now. But she saw no one approaching, heard no one calling her name. She was weakening. She didn't know how much longer she could hang on.

Icy solved that last problem for her. "I don't want to leave you hanging, so come on down—and chill!" Using her witchy magic, she brought Bloom down off the building and sent her crashing into the garbage cans below.

With an evil sneer and a wave of her arms, Icy sent ice crystals raining down. Soon Bloom was imprisoned in another one of the witch's fortresses.

Bloom coughed and tried to recover. Everything hurt—especially her ego. She was outnumbered, but the witches had kicked her around as if she were a defenseless rag doll. She should have been able to do something.

"So, you're a fairy," Icy sneered. She put her fingers on the ice and scratched deep lines into it. The screeching sound was like fingernails on a blackboard. "Well, we're the Trix."

Suddenly, Icy's hand froze.

"Hey! Leave our friend alone!" It was Stella. Standing with her were Musa, Tecna, and Flora.

Icy raised one eyebrow. "Seriously?" she said. Looking bored, she raised an arm and turned to the ogre. "Knut! Attack!"

It was a command the ogre seemed happy to obey. He flung himself at the four fairies. Just as he was about to barrel into them, the fairies moved out of the way. Knut went flying down the alley and landed with a grunt in a pile of trash cans.

The fairies regrouped in an instant. They were ready for battle!

"Magic Charmix!" they called out.

Bloom watched, astonished, as one by one, her roommates sprouted fairy wings and sparkling outfits, just as Stella had done back in Gardenia. They radiated light. One by one, they shouted:

"Stella! Fairy of the Shining Sun!"

"Flora! Fairy of Nature!"

"Musa! Fairy of Music!"

"Tecna! Fairy of Technology!"

Although Tecna had announced herself last, she was the first one to action. "Static Sphere!" she called out, and at once, Knut was encased in magical bubble. The ogre was trapped.

"Sonic Blast!" shouted Musa. A set of enormous speakers appeared and blasted a noise that was so loud, the vibrations broke the bubble. Knut was left hanging in the air.

Next, Flora summoned her own special powers. "Super Pollen!" she commanded. Bloom's eyes widened. Was Flora going to send Knut into a fit of sneezes? She had misjudged her roommate, though— Flora had something much bigger in mind. Magic swirled around her, and tiny white motes of pollen spun through the air. They gathered on the ground and re-formed into a magic vine—the same kind of vine Bloom had accidentally stepped on hours before. The vine shot up and grabbed Knut by the ankle.

The ogre howled.

The creeper began to twist up and around him, from ankle to head, until Knut was captured in a coil of vine. It squeezed him into a sausagelike shape and then tossed him away.

Though she was still helpless and trapped, Bloom felt a surge of pride for her fairy friends. Using their powers, they had easily taken care of the horrendous ogre!

The three witches were momentarily taken aback at the ogre's defeat. But Icy shrugged. "What a blockhead!" she grumbled. Then she narrowed her eyes menacingly at the four fairies, who stood defiantly in front of the witches. "You silly little fairies. You asked for it!" She lifted the edges of her cape and released a shower of arrow-shaped shards of ice. They flew through the air toward the fairies.

Tecna sprang into action. She summoned a magic shield and told her friends, "Hide behind me!" Then she called out, "Firewall!" The shield blazed with intense heat.

Icy's arrows were no match for Tecna's shield. As soon as they hit it, they dissolved into little wisps of smoke.

"Grrrr!" said Stormy. "Sisters, I'll take care of this!" She rose into the air and hovered above the fairies, then raised an arm and sent three blasts of energy down. The blasts were powerful enough to shatter Tecna's shield.

Icy smirked. "And I will finish them off!" She paused, concentrating her powers into a pulsing ball of evil energy.

The fairies knew they had to get out of there—but Bloom was still a prisoner! They rushed to her side and focused their magic on the block of ice surrounding their friend. Within moments, the ice had melted and Bloom was free!

Stella glanced at Icy, who was smiling as she prepared to unleash her evil energy on the fairies. "I'll take care of this!" the golden fairy declared. "Ring of Solaria!" Stella cried, and turned her gold ring

Bloom thinks she is a perfectly normal girl—until the day she discovers she's really a fairy!

Stella is the Fairy of the Shining Sun.
She is the first fairy Bloom meets.
She invites Bloom to Alfea College,
a school for fairies-in-training.

Flora is the Fairy of
Nature and can
magically control all
kinds of plants. She
is warm-hearted and
generous.

Tecna is the Fairy of Technology. She is extremely rational and creates unique gadgets to help in all kinds of situations.

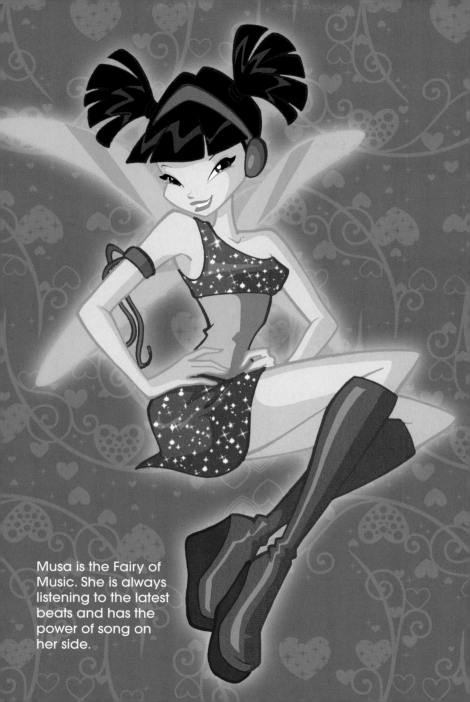

Musa is the Fairy of Music. She is always listening to the latest beats and has the power of song on her side.

Headmistress Faragonda runs Alfea College for Fairies. She is tough but fair, and is very protective of the fairies who attend her school.

The Trix are a trio of evil witches who are determined to destroy Bloom and her fairy friends!

Together Bloom and her friends make up the Winx Club. With their awesome fairy powers, there's nothing they can't do!

into the scepter. She swung the scepter into a broad circle, and a magical time-space tunnel appeared out of nowhere. "This will get us back to Alfea!" she told the other fairies.

"Oh, no you don't!" screamed Icy in disbelief.

"Girls, let's get out of here!" Stella commanded, and one by one, they jumped into the time-space passage.

Just before she leapt, Bloom looked over her shoulder. Icy released a powerful ray of evil energy that exploded and covered the whole city in a cold light. The witch looked satisfied until she realized it had all been for nothing. The fairies had escaped.

Stella's time-space tunnel delivered the five friends safely into their suite in Alfea. As they collapsed in the living room, Bloom breathed a sigh of relief. "Thanks for saving me from those witches!" she told her fairy friends, still shocked by the surprise attack.

Stella put a comforting hand on Bloom's shoulder. "I should have warned you about those three before we went to Magix City," she said. "Those witches call themselves the Trix and go to school at Cloudtower. They're always trying to get fairies into trouble."

"Well, I can't think of a more fitting name for them," Bloom said. "They're the most evil, tricky magical beings I have met so far."

Stella clapped her hands. "Hey! We should have a name," she exclaimed. "How about Stella's Team? Or the Stella Five?"

Flora groaned and Tecna gave a short giggle. Musa smiled, but she shook her head. Stella looked around the room. "No? What about"—a sparkle suddenly came to her eye—"the Stellairies! It's the best one yet!"

"The what?" Musa looked confused.

"Well, you know . . . ," Stella said, warming to her idea, "it rhymes with fairies!"

Musa frowned and shook her head no. "Nah. It sounds terrible!" The pigtailed Fairy of Music gave it a thumbs-down.

"How about . . . the Winx Club?" Bloom blurted.

The name had just popped into her head and out of her mouth.

Instantly, Flora raised her hand. "I vote for the Winx Club!"

Tecna and Musa chorused, "Me too!" Then Tecna, always the logical one, asked, "Uh . . . what does 'Winx' mean?

"Nothing!" Bloom giggled. "Just . . . us—the Winx!"

"I'll take the Winx over the Stellairies any day," Flora said with a laugh.

CHAPTER
10

In Magix City, the Winx had dodged real danger. Unfortunately, they couldn't dodge Griselda, who called them to her office the next afternoon. The headmistress's assistant had a job for them, and they weren't going to like it.

"Young ladies," Griselda said sternly, "it is a tradition at Alfea College that first-years take on a challenging task without the use of magic. And I have devised a very special task for you. Today, while the other students and teachers enjoy an outing, you will spend the entire day at school."

Bloom shrugged. Alfea was so exciting, she didn't mind staying at the college to take on whatever Griselda had in mind.

Griselda continued, "You will clean the castle from top to bottom!"

Flora was aghast. "The whole castle?"

"No, only the stairs, corridors, classrooms, and . . . bathrooms!" Griselda said with evident glee.

"Oh. No problem. I thought it was going to be much worse," Stella said with a sigh of relief.

Bloom tried not to giggle. With their magic, they would have the task done in no time!

Griselda clapped her hands. The noise was as loud as thunder. A glowing spark emerged from her palms. Griselda's magic had brought five buckets, each filled with a rag, soap, and detergent. Five mops, brooms, and scrub brushes appeared next. "You will find you have no access to your magic powers, so these are your work tools," she announced.

"What strange objects," Tecna said, firing up her handheld computer. "Let's see what my computer says about them."

Griselda was next to Tecna in a flash. She snapped the computer lid shut and warned, "You can't use technology, either!"

"Oh, snap, she got you!" Musa pointed at Tecna. The others laughed.

"It's not funny. You are being irrational," Tecna calmly told them.

"Young ladies!" Griselda interrupted. "Tomorrow I will conduct an inspection. Everything had better be clean. Now go!"

A short while later, Flora and Tecna stood at the foot of Alfea's grand staircase with the buckets and mops at their feet. Tecna wrinkled her brow.

"Do you want me to show you how?" Flora offered.

"That won't be necessary," said Tecna, lifting her chin proudly. "I'm sure I can figure out how to use these primitive instruments." She upended the bucket. A block of soap and a large rag fell out and tumbled to the floor.

"Are you sure?" Flora asked doubtfully.

Tecna grabbed the upside-down bucket and promptly put it on her head. She wasn't trying to be funny. She really didn't know what to do with a simple mop and bucket.

Flora started to laugh, but then she grew concerned when Tecna didn't remove the bucket from her head. "Are you really, really sure you don't want my help?"

"Of course!" Tecna replied. "I can handle the situation, Flora, don't worry—see?" She waited patiently, sure that at any moment the bucket would turn into a technical device that would allow her to complete the massive floor cleaning in front of them in the blink of an eye.

Flora gently removed the bucket from Tecna's head and sighed. "Oh, yeah, I see." She picked up a broom and handed it to Tecna. "Here, this is called a broom. You push it around the floor to gather all the dust and dirt into one pile."

Tecna accepted the broom and began to sweep the steps. Energetically, she put her whole self into it—and promptly knocked a painting off the wall. "I may have done something wrong," she sighed.

"Okaaay," Flora said. "Now do you want to let me help you?"

Meanwhile, Bloom and Musa were hard at work in a huge classroom. They had to clean everything—the desks, chairs, floors, walls, even the dust on top of the overhead lights! It was turning out to be an enormous, tedious task.

"Ugh! I can't wait to be finished," Bloom said.

"Yeah," Musa agreed. "We'd be done a lot sooner if you-know-who was helping us!"

She meant Stella. The blond fairy was perched on the teacher's desk, her legs crossed under her. Instead of holding a mop, a rag, or a broom, Stella was holding a mirror so she could admire herself.

Bloom shot Stella a look. "We agreed that you were going to clean the floors."

"No," Stella corrected them, taking out a nail file. "You two agreed. Hey, do you want me to break a nail?"

"We're breaking ours," Musa grumbled.

Stella raised her head royally and declared. "I'm a princess."

Bloom raised her head in surprise. "You're a

princess?" she asked the golden-haired fairy.

"Princess of Solaria," Stella replied smugly.

"So what?" Musa was unimpressed.

"So"—Stella raised her head regally—"I. Don't. Clean."

Observing this exchange gave Bloom an idea. It was only slightly mischievous. "I only see one way out of this," she said. Bloom poured a bunch of detergent and water into a bucket. Fluffy foam rose to the rim and spilled over.

"It's not fair!" Musa exclaimed to Bloom. "You shouldn't do Stella's work!"

Stella shrugged. "Well, somebody's got to do it." Filing her nails, Stella never saw the foamy suds coming at her until they landed—*splat!*—right on her face. "Hey!" she protested loudly.

Mission accomplished, Bloom dusted off her hands. "What were you saying, Stella?" she asked as she refilled the bucket.

Musa laughed heartily. "Good one, Bloom!"

"You think?" Bloom's eyes sparkled mischievously. "Well, I've got some for you, too!" With that, she flung a river of soapy water at Musa.

Musa ducked and narrowly avoided being soaked with the bucketful of suds. With a laugh, she raced to another bucket. She picked it up and aimed it at Bloom. "You're in for it, Bloom!" she yelled as Bloom dashed across the room. Bloom took cover behind a desk—only to be hit from behind by a well-placed toss of soapy water from Stella.

By the time Flora and Tecna found them, Bloom, Stella, and Musa were lying on the soapy floor, laughing so hard they could barely breathe.

"What happened in here, a tidal wave?" asked Flora, perplexed.

Stella waved her away. "Oh, we were just working some things out, right?"

"Right!" Bloom laughed.

"That's right," Musa chimed in.

Flora put her hands on her hips. "What a wreck," she declared. "We have to get this mess cleaned up!"

"We'll never finish this part," Tecna said, assessing

the size of the room and the extent of the damage that Bloom and her friends had done to it.

Bloom, Musa, and Stella gradually stopped laughing as they realized they still had a lot to do and the day was nearly over. Stella came up with a suggestion. "What do you say we ask the boys to join us?"

Bloom felt a shiver of excitement run through her. "The Specialists? Are they allowed into Alfea?" She thought about seeing Prince Sky again and her heart began to pound.

Stella nodded. "Of course they're allowed to come over! And I bet they'd love to help out. Furthermore, they'd get to spend time with me!"

Flora shook her head. "I don't think inviting the Specialists over is a very good idea. If we get caught by grumpy old Griselda, we'll be grounded until infinity."

Bloom sided with Stella. "I think it's a great idea! They could help us with the cleaning."

"But that's like cheating," Tecna said. "Isn't it?"

Bloom thought carefully. "No way," she said.

"Griselda said no magic, no gadgets. She didn't say no flesh and blood."

Stella was all over it. "Of course! And then when we're done cleaning, we can have a party!"

"That's a wonderful idea," chimed in Musa.

Bloom glowed. "I can't wait—yay!"

As it turned out, the Specialists thought hanging out with the Winx was a splendid idea. Brandon, Timmy, Riven, and Prince Sky roared up to the gates of Alfea on their flying motorcycles. When they hopped off, the fairies were there to welcome them. Bloom ran her fingers over Prince Sky's vehicle. "What do you call these?" she asked the prince.

"Wind Riders. They come in handy for just about anything," Prince Sky replied. His warm blue eyes rested on Bloom, and suddenly she felt she could barely breathe.

"Come along, you two. We have work to do!" said Flora. Prince Sky and Bloom guiltily turned their eyes away from one another and followed the rest of the Specialists and the Winx into the college and down a hallway that led to the large classroom that Bloom, Musa, and Stella had unsuccessfully tried to clean.

Once inside, the Specialists stood dumbfounded as Musa matter-of-factly told them they were there for a cleanup party that could not involve magic. She deftly demonstrated what to do with the mops and brooms that were lying around the classroom. "It's not hard. Just do it like this. Soap down, rinse, and dry."

"Um . . ." Brandon seemed confused.

"Huh?" said Timmy.

"But wasn't this supposed to be a party?" Riven complained.

"The party will start as soon as we finish cleaning," Bloom assured them. "Here, heads up!" She playfully tossed the mops and some cleaning supplies to the boys. Sky, Brandon, and Timmy caught them.

Riven did not. The mop tossed his way fell to the floor.

Ignoring him, Flora produced a CD player and

popped a disc into it. "We'll work better with music playing in the background."

"And . . . all together now: soap, rinse, dry!" cheered Musa.

Even though the Winx and the Specialists had their work cut out for them, the songs on the CD were catchy and put everyone in a good mood. The fairies and the Specialists got into it, cleaning to the beat.

Everyone, that is, except Riven. He stood to the side, muttering to himself.

In spite of Riven's nonparticipation, the Winx and the Specialists pulled it off. Alfea got cleaned much faster than it would have without the extra help.

As the girls were walking back to their suite with the Specialists, Bloom nudged Stella. "It went well, no?"

Stella agreed. "Everything's done. And I found out that Brandon is great with a mop." The princess-fairy impulsively leaned toward Bloom and whispered, "So, what's going on with you and Prince Sky?"

Bloom squirmed. "Uh, nothing."

"I saw the way you looked at him when he arrived on his Wind Rider. And I must say, the two of you would make a great couple."

"Really, Stella, nothing is going on between the two of us," protested Bloom.

"So why are you blushing?" Stella teased as they entered their suite. She gave Bloom an encouraging pat. "Anyway, this is the perfect time to get to know him."

Outside, night fell, beautiful and starry. Nearly all the students were away on the outing, and Alfea was dark except for the Winx's suite windows. The lights shone brightly as the Winx and the Specialists prepared to celebrate after a long day of cleaning.

Unbeknownst to them, though, there was trouble in the air. Three dark shadows swooped through the sky, making their way toward Alfea. When they arrived, the shadows circled the tower where the Winx were. It was the Trix! They were almost close enough to see inside.

"Didn't you say that the school was empty?" Darcy asked Icy and Stormy.

"Silly little fairies," Icy hissed. Her breath left little puffs in the air.

CHAPTER
11

Since the cleanup was finished, the party could finally begin! Bloom talked shyly to Prince Sky as Stella danced with Brandon. Timmy sat down next to Tecna. He motioned at the two who were grooving to the beat. "Don't you want to dance?"

"No, I don't like dancing," she told him. "It makes me feel kind of awkward."

"Well, that makes two of us," Timmy admitted with relief. "I don't like it, either. I feel ridiculous!"

Riven overheard Timmy's confession. "You're ridiculous even when you're not dancing," the surly teen grunted.

The best dancer, not surprisingly, was Musa, the

fairy of music. All eyes were drawn to her as she spun, shimmied, and moonwalked, tearing up the dance floor with her smooth moves.

"She's not bad, huh?" Sky whispered to Riven.

"Better than some others here," Riven reluctantly agreed.

As the night went on, the Winx and the Specialists talked and laughed and danced, having a blast. Even Riven started to loosen up after Musa asked him to dance.

Meanwhile, the Trix flew in close to the Winx's windows. Spying on the fairies was not the real reason they'd come to Alfea. But it was an added benefit.

"Let's conjure up the Vacuums," Icy commanded.

"The Vacuums—but why?" Stormy asked.

Darcy wrinkled her nose. "Sisters, I came with you because you said we were going to cause trouble in Alfea, which is my favorite thing to do. What's all this talk about Vacuums? What are they, and why are we looking for them?"

Icy gave Darcy an evil smile. "Vacuums are unique to witches, and dangerous tools, used only when absolutely necessary. They are foot-long swirling cylinders of light, conjured up on demand. Like heat-seeking missiles, or magical flashlights, Vacuums guide the users to hidden sources of magic. But they have an even better use. They can draw the magical energy out of one person and give it to another—and the energy can then be used for good or evil."

Darcy cackled with glee. "So you're trying to find a Vacuum that can trap the power of fairies and give that power to us?" She threw back her head and howled with delight. "How terrible. I love it!"

"We're looking for a powerful source of energy. I feel that the energy is somewhere in the school," Icy explained. "The Vacuums will take us to the source."

Using their dark powers, the witches managed to breech the magical walls of Alfea. "We will search this whole stinking castle for the Vacuums. We must succeed with our mission if we want to get back at those nasty fairies. But just in case those fairies come looking—" Icy motioned for Darcy and Stormy to join her. The three joined hands to form a small circle. At its center, a dark puddle bubbled. Slowly, the puddle expanded, rose up in the air—and reformed into a massive horned monster. A Minotaur!

"This should keep them busy!" Icy declared. The Minotaur roared angrily, and the Trix clapped their hands with delight. Leaving the Minotaur on the grounds next to Alfea to hunt the Winx, the three witches magically levitated through the floor and into the hallway. When the monster had disappeared down the corridor, Icy's evil eyes stared up at the ceiling. "The Vacuums must be this way," she said, rising up and motioning for the others to follow.

In the Winx's suite, the party was in full swing. Brandon was holding a glass for Stella to pour punch into when the glass started to shake. Stella spilled the punch all over the floor. "Brandon, are you nervous?" the mystified fairy asked.

"It's not me. It's the school that's shaking!"

Brandon was as surprised as Stella was.

"The shaking is coming from inside!" Flora said, walking over to them.

Stella frowned. "But I hear a loud noise coming from *out*side."

The group dashed to the terrace. "Maybe somebody left a TV on?" Stella ventured.

Boom! Another explosion rocked the building.

Stella shook her head. "Or maybe not."

In a flash, Riven was on it. He whistled, signaling for the Specialists' Wind Riders to appear. The boys flew off on their magic wheels to find out what was causing the trouble.

The Winx weren't about to let the boys have all the fun. The five fairies ran outside and across the courtyard, trying to figure out what was happening.

Damage.

That was the answer.

Someone—or something—had brought down one of Alfea's walls, which left a crater in the ground. The Specialists and the Winx huddled around the huge black hole.

"What kind of creature would do this?" Timmy asked in horror.

"A big, heavy creature!" Tecna said.

"Oh, golly. I never would have guessed," Riven said sarcastically.

Tecna took out her handheld computer. She punched in a couple of numbers and reported, "It's a little more than eight feet tall, and weighs close to a ton. Its fur is rather bristly. It has horns and multiple clawed limbs. It also has a musky odor. Now, is that better?"

"Way to go, Tec!" Stella cheered.

"What are we waiting for?" Brandon said, getting charged up. "Let's go!"

"Wait for us!" Bloom cried out as Brandon and Timmy zoomed into the black hole. Riven looked at Bloom.

"We're coming, too!" she declared.

Riven frowned, but Prince Sky accepted Bloom's offer. "Come on!" he urged.

Riven objected. "Stay where you are, little fairies!" he said. "This isn't a job for you."

Musa stepped up to him. "Says who?"

Tracking down the destructive monster took the two groups through all the halls and classrooms of Alfea. After a while, the Winx and the Specialists agreed to split up and hunt for the monster in two groups, to save time. "We'll give a shout if we find it," Bloom promised Prince Sky as they separated.

The Specialists soon found themselves in a darkened classroom. Brandon asked Timmy, "Why don't you give us some light?"

"Sure thing," the carrot-topped specialist agreed, using his ray gun to illuminate the room.

"It went up that way!" Brandon pointed at the ceiling, where a gaping hole was now exposed.

Out in the hallway, Musa led the Winx. "Let's try this way!" She headed off down a hallway to their left, then screeched to a stop. "Hang on a sec—there never used to be a wall in this corridor!"

It wasn't a wall.

It was the monster. It was so enormous, it blocked the entire hallway. The Minotaur roared, shaking the walls. Tecna, Flora, Musa, and Bloom jumped back, surprised and scared.

But Stella was not going to be frightened of a magical monster. The Fairy of the Shining Sun was merely annoyed. "This is totally disgusting," she said.

Bloom advanced, ready to cover for Stella. But when she tried to send a jolt of fairy magic toward the monster, nothing happened. Suddenly, she remembered and cried, "Stella! We have no powers! Griselda took them from us when she made us clean Alfea without magic!"

Realizing that without their magic they were in real danger, the Winx fled down a corridor, hoping to outrun the monster. The humongous shadow covering them proved they were failing. Tecna turned a corner to get out of the Minotaur's way, with Bloom hot on her heels. Flora ran with Stella in another direction, hoping to distract the monster from Tecna and Bloom, but suddenly the Fairy of Nature stumbled and fell flat on her face! There was no time to waste. Stella turned to her friend. She grabbed Flora's arm, lifted her up, and dragged her around the corner to safety.

Unfortunately, that safety was temporary. The monster ran full force at the two fairies.

The Minotaur was almost upon them when Stella got a gleam in her eye. "I have an idea!" she cried. "Wait here," she told Flora, pushing the fairy into a classroom and out of danger. Stella ran back around the corner and came face to face with the enormous beast. She stuck out her tongue and baited the Minotaur. "You are one nasty critter. Maybe this will freshen you up!" Then she ran toward a wall. As expected, the boulder-sized beast followed, with gathering speed. Just as Stella was about to smash into the wall, she hung a quick left, avoiding a collision.

The monster wasn't so nimble. It flew headfirst into the wall, puncturing it with its horns. The Minotaur howled as it shook its head back and forth, trying to dislodge its horns. The bumbling creature was stuck!

Just then, Bloom, Musa, and Tecna dashed into the hallway and came upon Stella and the Minotaur.

Tecna grimaced. "Great, you made it even angrier!" The Fairy of Technology had a point. It didn't take long for the Minotaur to free itself and come roaring back at them.

However, Stella's ploy had given the Specialists time to catch up. Riven raced into the room. "I'm going to take this thing down!" he promised.

Brandon, Timmy, and Prince Sky agreed.

"Let's take it on together," Sky declared.

"Why? I've got this covered," Riven boasted—even as the monster struck him first, which sent the maroon-haired Specialist flying. Riven crash-landed in the next room and lay on the floor, knocked out.

He wasn't alone for long.

Brandon, Timmy, and Prince Sky had raced to help Riven. Unfortunately, they proved to be no match for the Minotaur. It was having a field day with the Specialists, giving them a thorough trouncing. It grabbed Brandon in one of its massive fists and flung him hard against the wall. Timmy tried to attack the monster with his ray gun, only to be swatted away like a bag of feathers. The Minotaur then lowered itself so its horns were pointed straight at Prince Sky. Then it charged.

The Winx joined together. "We've got to do something!" Bloom said anxiously.

"The monster's beating them to a pulp!" Flora groaned.

"We don't have anything to fight him with," Tecna noted.

"Look what I found!" Resourceful Stella sashayed into the room bearing weapons—the brooms, buckets, mops, and other cleaning supplies the Winx and the Specialists had used only hours before.

"And I know just what to do with them!" said Bloom.

Flora, Musa, and Tecna understood. Without a word, the five fairies poured soap into the buckets and mixed furiously until a thick foam formed at the top of each one.

Just as the monster was about to clobber Prince Sky, it heard voices coming from another direction.

"Hey, monster!" called Bloom.

"We're he-ere!" Stella sang out.

The Minotaur was big and brawny, but it didn't have a lot of brains. It didn't realize it was being baited. It turned away from the boys and charged the Winx.

"Are you ready?" Bloom asked her friends.

"You betcha!" Musa answered for all of them.

The girls ran away with their buckets, forcing the monster to chase them. As they dashed down the hallway, they left a trail of the soapy concoction they'd mixed up.

The monstrous Minotaur slipped and went down hard, but it kept going! Then it slid out of control— and crashed through a window, falling, falling, falling, until it hit the ground below with a huge thump and lay still. It was out cold.

The fairies thought it was a good time to get a look at the thing. They trooped outside.

"What is it?" Flora asked the question that was on everyone's lips.

"It's horrible," Musa said.

"What I want know is where could a thing like

that have come from?" Bloom asked. She paused. "And what if there are more of them?"

Tecna stepped forward. "We've got to figure out what's going on."

Stella knew. "I'd say this is a special gift from the Trix 'R' Us company!"

Bloom thought it through. If Stella was right, that meant the Trix had somehow snuck into Alfea and conjured up this beast to distract, or take out, the Winx and their friends.

But how could they find out whether the crafty crew was really there? Even if the Winx searched the whole castle from top to bottom, the witches could easily stay out of sight.

"We need to know if the Trix are behind this, and if they're still in Alfea," Bloom declared. "They could be up to some really terrible tricks."

Stella said breathlessly, "Let's to go Headmistress Faragonda's office! She has a crystal ball that she uses to keep watch over the whole school. We can use it to find the Trix!"

"What exactly does Faragona's crystal ball do?" asked Bloom.

"It's a magical device that can tell you pretty much anything about what is going on," Tecna explained.

"But that wouldn't be right," Flora reminded them. "We can't go into Headmistress Faragonda's office if she isn't in there."

"That's true! I'm sure that's against the rules," Tecna added.

Bloom thought for a moment. "Yes, it's true that we would be going against the rules. But I think it's more important to find out what the Trix are up to, and only we can do it. Right now we are the only fairies at Alfea, and we must do everything we can to protect it."

Chapter 12

The Winx rounded up the Specialists and nervously made their way to Headmistress Faragonda's office. Outside her door, no one moved. It was up to Bloom to take the lead. "We have to go in," she said decisively, turning the knob and opening the door. It was pitch-black inside.

Riven took one step in, and he instantly sensed something. "Something's coming!" he whispered to the others.

"What if it's another monster?" Flora whispered. Her face showed her fear.

"What should we do?" Musa whispered to Bloom.

"Hide!" Bloom said. The Winx and the Specialists dove behind the desk.

From their hiding spot, they saw an incredible sight. The Trix didn't bother to use the door to the headmistress's office. They entered magically through a wall.

"This is odd," Icy said, staring at the whirling magical tool she had conjured up. "The Vacuum clearly indicates that the power of the Dragon Flame is hidden in this room. But I don't see anything." She shrugged her broad shoulders. "I guess we'll just have to trash the place and search every nook and cranny until we find what we want."

So that was it! Bloom realized. Stella was right. The monster had been conjured up by the Trix. But the witches-in-training had not come to Alfea to mess with the Winx. They had something much bigger on their sneaky minds. Bloom didn't know what the "vacuum" was, or exactly what the witches had come to steal. But with every fiber of her being, the newest fairy knew one thing: it wasn't happening on her watch. She boldly stepped out of her hiding place.

"Not so fast. We won't let you trash the head-mistress's office!" Bloom's voice rang out.

Riven jumped up, whirled around, found the light switch, and flicked it on.

Icy was not amused. "What are you doing here?" she demanded.

"No, what are *you* three doing here?" Bloom retorted.

"And that's what I was going to ask *all* of you!" Another voice cut the tension. It didn't belong to any of the teenagers.

Headmistress Faragonda herself was there!

A collective gasp filled the room. No one had expected this. And no one felt very brave as they faced the unsmiling headmistress.

Miss Faragonda's voice was steely. "Up until a moment ago, I thought this was *my* office."

Bloom blurted, "You might not believe us . . . but we can explain!"

The headmistress shook her head sternly. With a wave, she dismissed the Winx and the Specialists. Once outside, the boys summoned their wheels. Whatever consequences the girls were about to face, it was no longer the boys' battle. They powered up their bikes.

"Well . . . thanks for everything, Sky," Bloom offered.

Sky smiled. "It was an evening I won't soon forget," he said.

"Come here," Brandon said, crooking a finger at Stella. As soon as she got close enough, he surprised her with a smooch!

To Tecna, Timmy managed to say, "A memorable party!"

Riven's parting words were gruff. "The next time you girls have a party, don't invite me!"

Before they left, the Specialists took care of one more thing. They magically created four sturdy ropes. Then they wrapped the ropes around the Minotaur, imprisoning the still-unconscious beast, and hauled it away.

Meanwhile, Headmistress Faragonda was dealing with the break-in. She summoned her assistant to join her. "Griselda, remind me to send Director Saladin a letter of thanks for the help his students gave us." She then turned to the intruders: the Trix. She reprimanded them. "And as for you three young witches-in-training, I will immediately take this matter up with Headmistress Griffin. Your behavior this evening was totally unacceptable."

Icy frowned.

"Tomorrow morning," Headmistress Faragonda continued, "Headmistress Griffin will receive a formal complaint from me. I have never seen such a complete lack of respect. I trust that you will be disciplined accordingly."

Three pairs of eyes stared at the floor.

"Goodbye, girls," Miss Faragonda said, dismissing them with a little magic of her own. The Trix turned into silhouettes of light—and disappeared.

Griselda went outside to summon the Winx. "And now it's your turn," she said. Her voice gave nothing away. The Winx couldn't tell how much trouble they were in. They went inside to face Miss Faragonda.

"Now," their headmistress said, clearing her throat, "I've looked at the situation as a whole." She paused, and her eyes lit upon one fairy, then the next, down the line. She seemed to make up her mind right then. "So I will not discipline you."

"Whew!" Flora's sigh of relief filled the room.

Bloom's eyes widened. Was it possible to not be in trouble for this at all?

"This evening's events have shown me that you can handle difficult situations intelligently, creatively—and without magic. So I'll give you back your powers. You have acquitted yourselves admirably."

The minute they left the office, a cheer went up—and five pairs of hands did a series of high fives. Headmistress Faragonda was not going to punish them. And she had actually recognized their heroics!

As they celebrated, Stella giggled. "It's a good thing Headmistress Faragonda will never know that we were about to use her crystal ball!"

CHAPTER 13

That night, Bloom snuggled under the covers and drifted into a contented sleep. The next thing she knew, she was far from her room in Alfea and outdoors, surrounded by total darkness. She couldn't make out a street, a house, a tree, a moon, or a sky. But she could hear something—or someone.

"Blo-o-o-om," a musical voice sounded.

"Who's calling me? Who's there?" Bloom asked. The voice—a woman's, or a girl's—was familiar, but she couldn't place it.

Lost and alone, Bloom lurched forward in the dark, trying to feel her way by touch but finding nothing.

"It's me, Bloom. Do you remember me? Do you know my voice?"

It was coming from behind her now. Bloom whirled around, her arms out in front of her. "Who are you? What do you want?" Bloom cried, hobbling forward.

"Yes, Bloom! Come to me. . . . Come . . ."

"Where are you?"

"I am here!" the voice answered.

Something soft grazed Bloom's hand. She looked up. A vision of a woman bathed in light hovered above. Bloom squinted to see better, but the light grew in intensity. She had to turn away and shield her eyes. She never actually saw a face, or the arms reaching out to her.

"I'm waiting for you. . . ." The voice was starting to fade away, and Bloom strained to hear it. "Come to me. . . ."

Bloom grew frightened.

"And remember!"

"Remember? What do I have to remember?" Bloom pleaded for an answer.

The voice weakened. Bloom tried again. "What? What do I have to remember?"

The next voice she heard was Flora's. "That today is our first time in the Simulator!"

Bloom bolted upright in bed, and her eyes flew open. Confusion muddled her brain. She blinked, trying to get her bearings.

"Did you have a bad dream last night?" Flora guessed.

Bloom's sweet roommate was standing over her, dressed and ready to leave. Embarrassed, Bloom flushed as it dawned on her: she *had* been dreaming. She'd never had such a bizarre dream that had seemed so real. It hadn't been a nightmare at all. It had seemed so urgent, so . . . important. But why? Bloom had no clue.

Flora wore a look of real concern now.

"No, I'm fine. Thanks, Flora," Bloom assured the Fairy of Nature.

"Well, today is a big day," Flora said. "The Simulator is a real challenge."

"What's the Simulator?" Bloom asked as she sat up in bed and rubbed her eyes.

"It's a virtual reality room," Flora explained. "You go in and experience a virtual world. Apparently, everything feels so real, a lot of students forget it's an illusion."

So real. Just like Bloom's dream. She shivered. Her dream had felt chillingly real.

Okay, Bloom thought. Time to shake it off and get yourself together. It was her second day at fairy school, and she wasn't about to be late for class. She tossed off the blanket and flung her legs over the side of the bed. "I'll be ready in a minute," she told Flora. "I just wish I could really use my powers, be a real fairy."

"You'll be fine, Bloom. When you need your powers, they'll be there," Flora assured her.

Beneath the bed, a gray-and-white bunny peeked out. As soon as Bloom wasn't looking, Kiko hopped inside her backpack.

The lesson on the Simulator was held in the

computer room. Professor Palladium, an elfin teacher with long hair and pointy ears, stood by a huge control panel. Among its dials, levers, and switches was the big-screen monitor and keyboard of the supercomputer that controlled the Simulator. Above the control panel, a one-way mirror spanned the entire wall. It allowed the class to see inside the Simulator.

A dozen student fairies, including Bloom's roommates, were in the class. Standing in a semicircle around the teacher, they buzzed with excitement—until Professor Palladium asked for a volunteer.

"For this test," the professor explained, "you'll have to cast spells in a virtual place. Who wants to go first?"

Flora shrank back. "There's no way I'll be the first to go in there," she whispered.

Musa nudged Stella. "Stella, you always like to go first."

Stella shook her head vigorously. "Not this time. I've heard too many horror stories."

The professor held up a forefinger. "It seems as

though none of you want to try the Simulator. Very well, then. I'll choose a volunteer."

Stella, Musa, Flora, and Tecna huddled together, hoping he wouldn't pick one of them.

He didn't.

He chose Bloom.

All eyes turned to her. Bloom's mouth formed a giant O. A million thoughts raced through her head. What if she failed? What if her first demonstration as a student in Alfea turned out to be a disaster? Everyone would see her. The headmistress and teachers would realize they'd made a mistake in accepting her into a college for fairies. But as Bloom stood, she knew she *couldn't* fail. She owed it to herself to prove that she could be just as good as any of the other fairies in the school.

The smiling professor was waiting.

Trying hard to calm her nerves, Bloom slowly walked toward him.

"You can choose the environment," he said. "Which would you like?"

Bloom thought. She wanted to choose a place

that would show the other students in the class that she wasn't afraid of a challenge. As a number of places whirled through her mind, the image of a desert suddenly popped up. It was the perfect place to test her mettle—she'd have to make magic in a world that was dry, sandy, and hot. "I'm thinking of a desolate place," she heard herself say. "The most desolate place possible."

"Okay!" said the professor. "There's a place called Domino."

Bloom's eyes were on her teacher. Behind her, Kiko peeked out of her backpack but decided it was best to stay put.

"Your task is to try to improve your environment," Professor Palladium instructed.

Bloom steeled herself, took a deep breath, and timidly followed the professor to the Simulator.

"As soon as you enter the Simulator," the professor said, "Domino will materialize around you. Are you ready?"

Not really, Bloom wanted to say. But she couldn't exactly back out of her first task in a classroom! How would that look? Bloom glanced over her shoulder and gave her friends a wink. In turning, she noticed her backpack on the floor. What if she needed something inside it during her virtual visit to Domino?

"Oh, my backpack! Can I take it with me?" she asked the professor.

"Sure, take whatever you need," he replied.

Bloom went to get it.

Professor Palladium carefully opened the door to the Simulator. Beams of light radiated out. "There, Bloom. You'll have thirty minutes. I will be controlling everything," he assured her. "Now, do your best."

"I will," Bloom promised.

"Good luck," Musa called out, giving her friend a thumbs-up.

"You'll do great!" Flora cheered.

"Have a good time," Stella said with a wave.

"Figure it out!" Those were Tecna's parting words.

Stella nudged the Fairy of Technology. "What kind of encouragement is that?"

"The most rational kind," Tecna answered.

"Thanks, Winx! See ya!" Bloom called back to

her friends. It hit her that there were two possible outcomes to today's class. She'd either flunk miserably in front of everyone—or she might actually do okay. She wasn't counting on a third option when she closed the door behind her.

CHAPTER
14

Bloom took tiny steps along a walkway suspended across the top of the Simulator. It was the only way in. Panels of amber lit up one after the other until the circular room was aglow. It was kind of cool, Bloom had to admit.

Then the walkway retracted under her feet and left her stranded in midair. That wasn't so cool! Sure she was about to drop like a rock, Bloom shut her eyes and opened her mouth to scream. When two seconds went by and she hadn't fallen, she opened one eye.

Bloom was still suspended in the air!

When her feet finally did hit the ground, it was onto rocky, parched earth. Everything was dusty and brown and dry. The ceiling above had transformed into a collection of clouds. There wasn't a living thing in sight.

So this is Domino, Bloom thought. It was the desolate landscape she'd asked for, a choice she was beginning to regret. This place, real or not, was creeping her out. Bloom pulled her backpack close and forced herself to concentrate on the assignment. She wanted to get out of Domino and out of the Simulator as soon as possible.

"Now, what can I do to improve this place?" she wondered aloud. She decided to look in her backpack to see if anything might give her an idea. She stuck her hand in and was surprised to touch something soft, fluffy, and moving!

Kiko!

"What are you doing here?" Bloom asked as her pet hopped onto the arid earth. Kiko wiggled his ears happily. Even though he had jumped into a strange, alien world, he was perfectly content to be with Bloom wherever she was. Bloom didn't know if pets were even allowed in the Simulator! But it was too late now.

As Kiko hopped around, sniffing at the strange environment, a thought occurred to Bloom. When she had left for Alfea, she had packed some seeds for Kiko as a snack. They were still in her backpack.

"I'll start with a few seeds and see if I can make them grow," Bloom said. She reached into her backpack and rummaged around until she found a little pouch. Inside the pouch were Kiko's seeds.

"Bingo!" Bloom exclaimed. She dug into the dirt and planted the seeds, careful to cover them with the right amount of soil.

Okay, she thought, now it's time to see if I have the right magic. She placed her hand over the small pile of dirt that covered the seeds, and concentrated hard. "Grow, little ones! Sprout!" she whispered into the earth.

Then Bloom watched, amazed, as an intense blue light came from her fingertips. Was this her magic, here when she had summoned it? After a few seconds, Bloom lifted her palm. A small but definitely green shoot poked through the ground.

"Oh, good!" Bloom said. She had done it! It wasn't

the biggest magic deal ever, but it was something. A good start, she praised herself. She hoped the people outside the Simulator, Professor Palladium and the Winx and the rest of her classmates, agreed. If she was lucky, maybe the professor would think she had done enough and end the simulation. Domino was not a planet that Bloom wanted to visit again.

But she was about to find out that she would not be so lucky.

In a darkened room deep in Cloudtower, the Trix were planning their next move. The Winx had defeated them at Alfea, but the witches were not about to give up on capturing the massive source of energy they had detected within the fairy college.

"What if we got the Specialists to be on our side?" suggested Darcy. She used her magical ability to do some calculations on the Specialists. "Interesting. Riven has a very strong negative force." She turned to her clique. "He's on the same level with us! What do you think?"

"Not impressed," said Stormy. "You're wasting time. None of the Specialists can be turned. Those silly, sparkly outfitted fairies have them wrapped around their little fingers."

Icy raised a hand, indicating she did not agree with Stormy. "Riven could be useful. But not yet. We'll think about it later."

Darcy bent her head to concentrate. After a moment, she lifted it triumphantly Using her witch powers, she had been able to locate something. "Trix! The source of power we were looking for last night is in the Simulator at Alfea!" She furrowed her brow in concentration and then gasped. "I can see Bloom there right now!" she declared.

"Sisters, let's pay a visit to the Simulator," Icy said to Stormy and Darcy. "First, I'll mess with the Simulator so it can't be turned off. Next, we follow the Vacuum to the power!" Her eyes brightened. "It's possible that Bloom has the power of the Dragon Flame within her—but we'll need to make sure," Icy muttered under her breath. She gathered her powers and flashed an evil smile as she cast a spell on the

Simulator. Then all three witches summoned their powerful Vacuums. With howls of laughter, they transported themselves right into the Simulator.

Bloom's friends, watching through the one-way mirror, saw the intruders first. "The Trix!" the Winx gasped.

"Bloom is in danger," Tecna told the professor. "There are three witches called the Trix who will stop at nothing to destroy her!"

Professor Palladium paled. "Let's get her out immediately!" The elfin teacher didn't waste any time. He pounded away at the console in the computer room. The Winx grew uneasy as they watched. With every passing second, he seemed more tense and frustrated. "What's going on?" he cried. "Someone has tampered with the Simulator!" He tapped frantically at a few more buttons, but Bloom remained inside. Soon she would have to deal with the Trix. It would be three against one, and Bloom had yet to test her fairy powers.

Stella, Musa, Flora, and Tecna exchanged a look of fear.

Professor Palladium realized he could not save Bloom—the spell on the Simulator was too strong. All that he, the Winx, and the rest of Bloom's classmates could do was watch helplessly as the Trix moved in on the unsuspecting fairy.

CHAPTER
15

With Kiko at her side, Bloom went about exploring Domino, looking for something else she could do to improve it. She had no seeds left, but she thought maybe she would find something living in the barren world that she could nurture and help to grow. Suddenly, she heard a voice behind her that sent a chill down her spine.

"Hey there, junior fairy!"

Bloom spun around, her heart in her throat. Either her eyes were playing tricks on her, or the actual Trix had broken into her virtual world.

She blinked and moved toward them for a closer look. Icy, Stormy, and Darcy hung suspended in the air. Apart from that, they seemed real enough. "What are you doing here?" Bloom asked.

"We just thought we'd drop in," Darcy sneered. The green-hued witch paused and raised an arm to conjure up some magical mischief. "We wanted to give you a little encouragement!" She laughed.

Bloom backed up, scared now—with good reason. She had already fought against the Trix once, in Magix City, and she knew her powers weren't strong enough to defeat them by herself. As Bloom looked for somewhere to run, Darcy hurled stinging rays straight at her.

Luckily, Bloom jumped away in the nick of time. With a sick feeling, she realized there were no trees or bushes, no signs of life—no hiding places in Domino. All she could do was keep moving and hope that the Trix's dark magic missed her. She somersaulted away from them and landed on her knees.

"Enjoy!" Stormy was the next one to taunt Bloom. The witch with wild weather powers fired off her magic. She wasn't aiming for Bloom, though. Stormy sent her lightning bolts straight into the ground. She knew exactly what she was doing.

To Bloom's horror, the earth beneath her cracked. With each bolt from Stormy, more cracks appeared, each one wider than the next. A burst of scalding steam rose from underground, forcing Bloom backward. She found herself trapped on an island between boiling bursts of steam. And it was about to get worse. Stormy's next target was Bloom herself.

Lightning struck just inches from her feet, and then—*boom!*—a big explosion sent Bloom rocketing into the air. She came down hard.

That did it! Bloom went from fearful to furious. "I've really had it with you girls!" she shouted at her tormentors. She was ready to fight back. Icy's next words sent her stomach plunging.

"Look what we found—a bunny!"

Bloom whirled around. Kiko was trapped on a rock, surrounded by deep gouges in the earth. Steam was rising from below him. The rabbit trembled.

Bloom didn't know how she could get to him.

When she looked down to see if she could jump over the rising vapor, what she saw struck panic in her heart. Red-hot lava boiled in cracks in the earth.

"Kiko!" Bloom screamed. "Don't move!"

"Rabbits are vermin," Icy said coldly. "So let's get rid of it!" She aimed a magic ray at Kiko. It smashed the rock beneath his feet to bits. With nothing solid to stand on, Kiko lost his balance and hurtled downward, straight toward the sea of scalding lava.

Without thinking, Bloom took a flying leap after him.

Icy cackled, "Ha, ha, ha, ha, ha! I guess she really *loooooooves* that rabbit!"

Just outside the Simulator, Professor Palladium and the class watched in horror.

"Professor, do something!" Stella cried.

"An evil spell is interfering!" the teacher said as he kept pounding away, trying to somehow unlock the computer and free Bloom.

Stormy and Darcy circled above, watching Bloom plunge downward.

Only . . . something miraculous occurred as the

determined fairy plummeted toward certain doom. As she fell, Bloom's rage was so great, she thought she might explode.

Instead, magic happened.

Fairy wings sprouted on her back. Her ordinary school clothes morphed into a fierce fighting outfit. Bloom felt a surge of powerful energy. She stopped falling and began to fly fearlessly toward the flames to save Kiko. Nothing else mattered. Best of all, Bloom believed she could do this. She had truly transformed.

For the first time ever, the girl who had always believed she was a fairy became a fairy.

Only, she was not so much like the sweet and gentle sprites she used to read about. She was a real fairy, powerful and brave, ready and able to blast the bad guys—or girls, in this case—into another dimension.

A blinding light formed around her. Bloom rose from the black hole. She focused on the witches, who wanted to destroy Kiko. She felt a surge of new energy coursing through her veins and flowing out her fingertips. In a split second, Icy, Darcy, and Stormy were hit with a bolt of dragon-shaped magic so powerful, they had no time to fight back. Bloom's fiery fairy magic blasted them right out of the Simulator!

Once she was sure that the wicked Trix were gone, Bloom sank down, exhausted. As she hit the ground, her eyes closed and everything turned black.

The force of Bloom's magic booted the Trix all the way back to Cloudtower. It had happened so fast, and with so much force, that it took Icy, Stormy, and Darcy quite a while to catch their breath. Huddling together, the Trix planned their next move against Bloom and the rest of the Winx. They lost the battle in the Simulator, but they were determined to defeat Bloom and her fairy friends.

"That new fairy must be destroyed!" Darcy said, fuming. "Bloom has more power than the rest of the fairies at Alfea combined!"

Stormy nodded. "Bloom might be powerful, but we'll crush her little fairy wings eventually, just you wait." She turned to Icy. "Sister, did you find what you were looking for in the Simulator?"

"Yes! Yes! Yes!" Icy exclaimed. "It is Bloom! She has the power of the Dragon Flame!"

"What is that?" Darcy asked.

Icy smiled an evil, witchy smile. "Only the most powerful magic in all of the Magic Dimension." She raised her voice and spoke. "Sisters, if we can capture the Dragon Flame from Bloom using our Vacuums, we will have all of Magix at our command!"

When Bloom awoke, she was still in Domino. It took a moment for her to remember where she was and what had happened. She was in the Simulator, in Domino, a virtual place. Bloom surveyed the ruined landscape with despair. Her assignment had been to make the land better. But because of the Trix, Domino looked bleaker than ever. She had failed her assignment in front of the whole class! Then Bloom thought about Kiko. Her heart sank. She had tried so hard to save him. . . .

A familiar sound interrupted her thoughts. She sat up and looked around. A pair of rabbit ears peeked out from behind a rock.

"Kiko?" Bloom was almost afraid to say her pet's name. She got up and moved closer. Long pointy ears were rising and falling. They were accompanied by the sound of—snoring?

Bloom rushed toward the sound. And there he was, her beloved bunny, unharmed—and asleep! She had saved him after all!

"Kiko!" Bloom cried.

The rabbit jolted awake. Then he hopped right into Bloom's arms.

Bloom held him tight. "I thought you were . . . Oh, KIKO!"

Outside the Simulator, Professor Palladium finally broke the evil spell that had trapped Bloom inside. Bloom saw the door to the Simulator open, leading to the classroom. But Bloom didn't run out immediately. She needed to let it all sink in. She had fought off the evil Trix. She had transformed. Her powers had been there when she had really needed them. That was when Bloom finally believed the truth. "I'm a real fairy!" she said out loud.

Stella, Musa, Flora, and Tecna burst in and threw their arms around Bloom. They were followed by Bloom's classmates, who arrived screaming, cheering, whistling, and high-fiving. They lifted Bloom high above their heads. All together, the fairies formed a trampoline and bounced Bloom high into the air, over and over again.

What a feeling! Bloom had been airborne before, but this, powered by all her friends—this was the real meaning of flying high! As she gazed upon the sea of celebrating fairies surrounding her, Bloom knew it was the happiest moment of her life.